WELCOME TO
PASSPORT TO READING
A beginning reader's ticket to a brand-new world!

Every book in this program is designed to build read-along and read-alone skills, level by level, through engaging and enriching stories. As the reader turns each page, he or she will become more confident with new vocabulary, sight words, and comprehension.

These PASSPORT TO READING levels will help you choose the perfect book for every reader.

READING TOGETHER
Read short words in simple sentence structures together to begin a reader's journey.

READING OUT LOUD
Encourage developing readers to sound out words in more complex stories with simple vocabulary.

READING INDEPENDENTLY
Newly independent readers gain confidence reading more complex sentences with higher word counts.

READY TO READ MORE
Readers prepare for chapter books with fewer illustrations and longer paragraphs.

This book features sight words from the educator-supported Dolch Sight Words List. This encourages the reader to recognize commonly used vocabulary words, increasing reading speed and fluency.

For more information, please visit passporttoreadingbooks.com.

Enjoy the journey!

Little, Brown and Company

Hachette Book Group
1290 Avenue of the Americas, New York, NY 10104
Visit us at lb-kids.com

Little, Brown and Company is a division of Hachette Book Group, Inc.
The Little, Brown name and logo are trademarks of Hachette Book Group, Inc.

The publisher is not responsible for websites (or their content)
that are not owned by the publisher.

First Edition: September 2016

Library of Congress Control Number: 2016940587

ISBN 978-0-316-35647-3

10 9 8 7 6 5 4 3 2 1

CW
•

Printed in the United States of America

Passport to Reading titles are leveled by independent reviewers applying the
standards developed by Irene Fountas and Gay Su Pinnell in *Matching Books to
Readers: Using Leveled Books in Guided Reading*, Heinemann, 1999.

Adapted by Jennifer Fox

Based on the episode "The Dignity of Teeth"

Written by Ben Gruber

L B

LITTLE, BROWN AND COMPANY

New York   Boston

Attention, Teen Titans fans!
Look for these words when you read
this book. Can you spot them all?

dolls

breath

cavity

money

"What is that smell?" yells Robin.
"Beast Boy's onion and garlic
stew," says Cyborg.

Robin gasps.

"Your breath is TOXIC, Titans!"

"You guys need to brush," Robin says.

The Titans get to work.

"Not your hair!" Robin cries.

"Your TEETH!"

Beast Boy opens his mouth wide.
"Look, a cavity!" Robin shouts.
"That tooth needs to go."

"No way," says Beast Boy.
"I love ALL my teeth!"

Cyborg tells Beast Boy
that the Tooth Fairy
brings money for teeth.

"A fairy...how sweet!"
says Starfire.
"I think it is creepy,"
says Raven.

That night, Beast Boy leaves his tooth under his pillow.

The next day he looks. "I got paid!" he cries.

He starts losing teeth on purpose to get more money.

The other Teen Titans see
Beast Boy's cool new sunglasses
and piles of money.

They start losing teeth
on purpose, too.

Raven still thinks that the Tooth Fairy is creepy.

Soon the Teen Titans look like toothless zombies. "More money!" they yell.

"That is it," Raven shouts.

"We are getting your teeth back."

The Tooth Fairy's lair
is full of teeth.

"Creepy!" Raven says.
The Tooth Fairy
flies into the room!

"What do you do with
all the teeth?" Raven asks.
"Make jewelry?" Robin guesses.

"Dress them up like dolls?"
asks Starfire.

"No, I EAT them!"
the Tooth Fairy says.

"Ew," Raven says. "Give my friends their teeth back!"

The Tooth Fairy makes
a deal with Raven.

"We will have a contest.
If you win, you get
your friends' teeth back.
If you lose, I get your teeth, too!"

"Fine," says Raven.

"What is the contest?"

"An eating contest!"
cries the Tooth Fairy.
"We will eat TEETH!"

Raven tastes a tooth.

"Wow," she says. "That is good!"

Raven shovels teeth in her mouth.

In a flash,
her pile is gone.
Raven wins!

The Tooth Fairy gives back
the Teen Titans' teeth.

At home, the Teen Titans
thank Raven for saving
their teeth.

"You were right," Cyborg says.
"You cannot put a price
on your teeth."

"No," says Raven...

"...but you can eat them!"